KATE

How To Win A Girl

NOT TO

KOUSAR (EDDY NEINSTEIN)

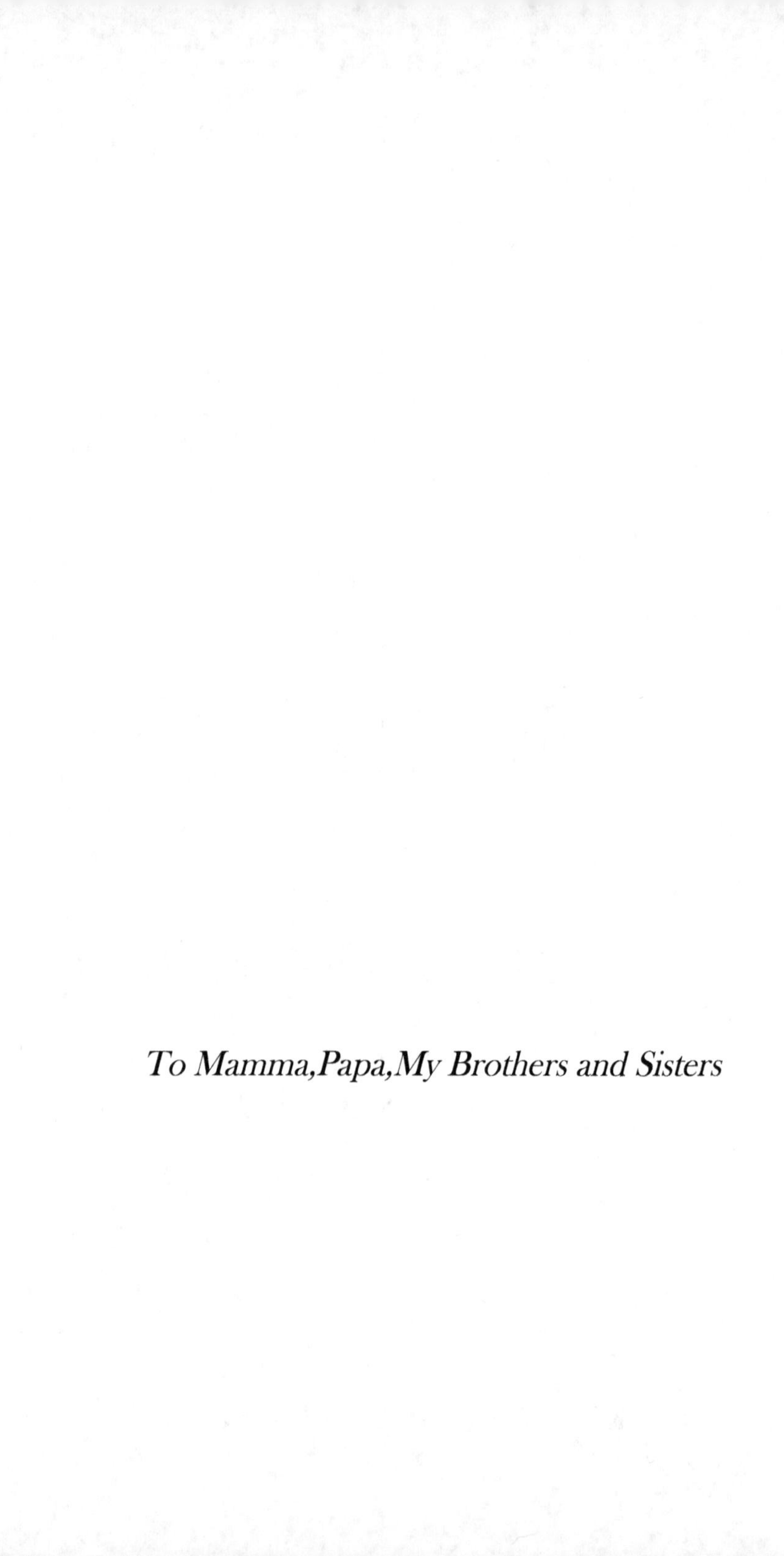

To Mamma,Papa,My Brothers and Sisters

*Special Thanks ! to my teachers
who made me the person i'm today.*

*I also want to thank my friends and
classmates for gifting me the beautiful
memories and their precious time.*

<u>PROLOGUE</u>

Alright! Let's do this.Let's start with an
introduction.My name is
Kousar and i'm from Jammu&Kashmir
(India).But you can call
me Eddy because my friends call me with this
name.I come from
a middle-class family and i'm pursuing a
Bachelor's in IT (last year).

The reason i'm writing this book is that
i just want to share my story
with this world.
I want to share my story with you.
I want you to judge me,
and most importantly i want you to learn
something from my story.

If this book helps just a single person out there,
just a single person ,

i would consider myself the
Happiest Person alive.

And one more thing
i just want to narrate the story as it is .

What i mean is that there is going
to be a lot of slang and a little swearing.
I just want it to be as pure as possible.So Let's
begin!

<u>Chapter 0 : New Faces</u>

'Yo! Do you know what's gonna happen today?,'
Jon said in excitement standing
beside me in our classroom.

'No!,' I replied combing my hair back with my
fingers.

Yes! I have a problem combing my hair with my
fingers ,thanks.

'You are dumb man , It's the first day of our new
classes ,' Jon said
placing his arm around my shoulders while
looking at the door with excitement.

'New kids are going to join us today bro,
new faces man,girls,
isn't that awesome?,' Jon said,
pushing me with his shoulder.

In Kashmir schools reopen after 3 months of winter vacations.Which start from December and end on 28th February.Most of the schools reopen on 1st March .

And the new admission or students join schools on the same day.

So
Jon was basically talking about new girls that were going to join our class that day.We were in 5th standard,you know 11 and 12 years old devils(I know what you are thinking ,so young and talking about girls?Well you know ,i guess guys start talking about girls when they get 10 year old.Don't blame us.
Almost all guys are bad boys.)

'Really?Look at these girls in our class man ,do you think you would like to talk to any one of them,' I said, pointing to the girls sitting on the benches in our classroom.

'That's what i'm tryna say man , it's new maal(stuff) bruh,just wait and watch,'
Jon replied still staring at the door with excitement.

Jon was one of the tallest students in our class.He had a fair complexion,and dimples formed in his cheeks whenever he smiled or laughed. Jon also stuttered a lot.

At that time i considered him as my best friend.He wasn't into girls that much but he would jump into the conversations anyways.

As we were waiting for the new students (i mean girls) to enter the class
our teacher came in and shut the door.It simply meant that no new students(girls) were going to join us for that year.I looked at Jon grumpily , he looked back with astonishment.We sat down on our benches hopelessly.

The first day after 3 long months was going to turn into a bad experience.It felt like we had lost a battle .We were getting bored with the girls in our class.We wanted something new.Every other class and sections had their own queens and angels .But in our class guys were the devils and girls,well we didn't even care what creatures they were.

'Goooood Morrrrrrning maaaam,' the whole class greeted the teacher, standing in their benches.

'Good morning, good morning sit down,' the teacher instructed the class.

'Thankkkkk Yoouu maaaam,' the class replied to the teacher.

I don't know why students here just stretch the words when they are greeting

teachers.It's kind of a universal problem here.

'Any new students today?,' teacher questioned the class.

'No mam,' the front row students answered quickly , like they were in a QnA show ,front row students are generally nerds (fact).

Guys were silent.Like someone had taken their lunch away(which they never ever brought with them,because they would eat from other student's lunches and most of the time left them nothing to eat).

'Ok! Let's start then,' the teacher said to the class.

As we were about to open our books , someone knocked the door.

'Hold on please ,' the teacher instructed the class .I was looking for my pencil in my bag and the teacher got up from her chair to open the door.

'Students,students,' Jon said pushing me gently with his elbow.
I looked at the door and 2 or 3 guys entered the class.

'New admission ?,' the teacher asked the students at the door .

'Yes mam,' answered the students.

'Get in,' the teacher said pointing to the class.

'What now ? These are just guys man, no girl, shut

up now?,' i said to Jon

The teacher started the first chapter , first page.As she finished the first paragraph.There was a knock on the door.
She got up again, headed to the door and opened it.
I looked up this time , glanced at the door and Boom! I'm blown away.

A girl entered the class.

As you might have guessed , there she was .The first love of my life.
I couldn't take my eyes off her.I couldn't help my self.I just kept staring at her.You should have seen her man.

She was wearing a blue skirt ,white shirt,white socks and black shoes.She had a fair complexion , little red chubby cheeks and had a boy's haircut. Her voice ,it was out of this world.Despite being a 11 year old kid i had an instant crush on her.I couldn't help myself.The teacher told her to sit on the bench at the front with other girl.

'Oiiiiiii! Look at her, ' Jon said delightfully.

I looked at Jon and we smiled .We knew what we had to do.Next mission .Get her name.

Chapter 1 : Hello! Neighbour

A week passed by and no guy knew her name.Because no guy had the guts to ask her name and no guy bothered to ask the other girls what her name was.Infact i guess there were 5-6 guys interested in her and the remaining guys were either shy or nerds.

'Man we gotta get her name .You are interested in her , why don't you go ask her name?,' Jon asked me

I had a crush on her and i wanted to know her name .But i had to play it cool.If Jon knew what im feeling for her , he would definitely ruin it all.He would rush to her and tell her that i had a crush on her.And i would never ever let that happen.I had to play safe.

'Who cares man?pffffffffff,' I replied like i didn't care.

'But we gotta have her name bro,' Jon said

Jon was doing it for the sake of fun .But i , i was thinking something else.
While we were discussing this super important matter, Saleem jumped in.

'Yo listen up man, you see that girl.The new girl.What's her name ?,' Saleem questioned us with excitement.

He hardly attended school.It was his first day after the vacations and he wanted to know her name as well.Great!

Me and Jon we looked at each other and an idea sparked in my mind.

I thought you know ,no guy has the nerve to ask
her name .Why don't we use Saleem as a bait?

'Her name ? ,' I said to Saleem

'Yeah man.What is it?,' Saleem asked in haste

'Pyari (meaning sweet or lovely in hindi),' I replied
with an evil smile.

'Wow! Lovely face , lovely name.Now just watch
me how i talk to her ,' Saleem said winking at us.

'It's going to be epic ,' I said to Jon .

As Saleem approached her.We got excited.We
knew it was going to get bad for poor Saleem.

'Can i get your copy(Here we say copy not notebook.Saleem was asking her for her notebook) Pyari?,' Saleem requested her.

'What did you just call me ?,' she asked.

'Pyari.Your name right ?,' Saleem replied nervously.

Shhhuuttttttt!!!
'It's not my name.Who told you that ?,' she asked after slapping Saleem.

Me and Jon were watching the whole scene and we were dying with laughter.

'Those two guys at the back ,' Saleem replied pointing towards us while rubbing his cheek with his hand.

She approached us with poor Saleem for inquiry.We were still laughing.

'Did you told him my name is Pyari? ,' she questioned me.

I had mixed feelings.I was excited because we were fiinally going to get her name.And at the same time i was nervous because i hardly talked to any girl
at that time.

But i wanted to make a good impression so i had to be confident and brave as well.

'Yes i did,' i said .

Jon and Saleem both watching me silently.

'Why?,' she asked.

I was confused.I thought if i told her that i wanted to know her name .She might think that i'm a bad guy who is after girls all the time or something else.I said to myself man honesty is the best policy.Give an honest answer.

'You look sweet and cute , that's why.And i don't know your name.So i thought let's call you the way you look , Pyari,' I said shrugging .

Saleem was still rubbing his cheek and Jon he was looking at her.She paused and smiled.

'It's Tamanna,not Pyari don't call me that ever again,' she said and smiled.

'Tamanna it is ,' I replied.

'Pyari ,stupid,' she said and we all laughed.

At that point i thought she might slap me as well.But it turned out that she was friendly and a positive person.

At that time i realised that you should never judge a book by it's cover.Knowing her name was not enough for me.I wanted to know her more and i felt like she wanted to know me too.But when it came to talking to girls.

I was a loser. At the same time i wanted to talk to her.I was a back bencher and she sat at front .There was 4-5 benches between us.I never even

tried to talk to her in free time not even in lunch time. I was nervous all the time but never told anyone.

Some more days passed by and i did nothing.All i knew was her name.

One day our teacher decided to shuffle the students.I was scared.I thought i might have to sit with some nerd.Me and Jon were the awesome duo.And i wanted to sit with him all the time.To my luck, the teacher left us alone .We were really happy and what added to my happiness was that the teacher made Tamanna sit next to our bench with this shy girl.

Again i had a lot of mixed feelings.I was super happy, super excited and above of all i was nervous.

I wanted to break the ice .But i didn't knew how? So i don't know i just went for it.

'Hey Neighbour , how are ya?,' I asked her leaning
a little towards her.

'I'm good.How are you?,' she replied and smiled.

'I'm fine,' I said.

I thought she might not talk at all.But it
worked.Now, i gained some confidence.I started
making some progress.

Chapter 2 : First Rejection

Since the day i talked to her for the first time, we were getting along very well.We were talking all the time.I was right about her.She was really friendly, free thinking, driven, smart , didn't gave a damn about anything or anyone.

I guess these are the qualities that almost every guy is looking for in almost every girl.Every day she was attracting me more and more.Everything was going smooth.We became really good friends.Whenever she entered the class,she would drop her bag (Here we say bag , not backpack) on her desk and come to us to greet us.Then we would talk until the teacher would get in the class.

Whenever we looked at each other in the class , we would smile at each other.I do admit that i had a crush on her from the very beginning.But i never ever thought of proposing her.I just wanted it to be the way it was.

Almost every student in the class thought that we were in a relationship.
It was crazy but i never cared about what anyone thought of us.For me we were good friends and nothing more than that.We had mutual feelings about each other.

'Man are you guys in a relationship?,' Jon asked me

'What do you think?,' I asked him.

'Yes you are .Everyone knows it.,' Jon said scratching his chin.

'We are not man, we are just friends that's it.Don't believe these girls and guys bro,' I replied spreading my arms .

'Come on ! Everyone knows it.Stop lying man.Saleem knows it,Baba knows it.Everyone does.Look at the way you guys talk to each other.You don't talk to anyone like that man.You guys are love birdies.I'm happy for ya man.You ma tiger,' Jon explained.

'We are not man, i swear.We are just friends thats it.Just good friends,' I insisted.

We went on arguing about it for almost 3-4 classes.But Jon, he would never listen.After lunch break we had a Games class.It was really a special class because only one or two classes would play in the ground .

You were free to do anything .A lot of students would play Cricket and girls usually formed groups and would gossip about stuff.And on that particular day , i don't know why no one was playing in the ground.There was a group of girls and a group of boys.This simply meant something was wrong.I was unaware of the situation .Me and Jon we were hanging out with the other guys.We had our own gang.

I felt uneasy.I felt like something was going to happen.Tamanna was with the group of the girls in the other side of the ground and me and my gang was on the other side.Little did i knew that there was a super rare, evil alliance between the boys and the girls.What they wanted? Well , you might have guessed it.

They wanted us (Me and Tamanna) to propose each other in front of everyone.I should have been wearing diapers at that day.It was impossible for me.I would have ran away but the boys had caged me.There was nowhere to go.

'You can do it man, don't be shy, what are you guys looking at lets take him to her,' Baba ordered evryone.

'Baba please don't do this man.We are just friends bro.Please,' I begged trying to pudh myself back.

'Naah! Don't act coward man.She won't eat you .Push him boys,' Baba instructed the group and laughed.

Every guy on back started pushing me forward.I tried my best to run but the group overpowered me.I had to do this.I had no other option left.On the other side , the girls were doing the same.As we got closer , i felt like crying.

I said to myself , just do it.

The girls were laughing and the guys were laughing as well.Their laugh was making me nervous.For them it was just a show.

'Say it man,' One of the guys from the group yelled.

'He... Hey....How are you?,' I stuttered still trying to escape.

'Hey Tamanna he wants to talk to you ,' someone shouted from the group.

'Would you people excuse us for a minute .I want to talk to him in person,' Tamanna ordered everyone .

It worked! Everyone walked away .

'Come here,' Tamanna said.

'Did you tell them that im your girlfriend?,' She asked .

She was frowning .I thought maybe it's the last day of our friendship.I thought i had lost it all.Everything was going perfect and everyone ruined it.

I was hopeless.

'No, i didn't. They were just forcing me .I didn't tell anyone

anything,' I replied nervously .

'Hmmmm! I see .Do you like me?,' She asked , her mood changed a little.

Questions started taking place in my mind.I thought maybe she really wants to be more than friends or maybe she wants to know what i feel for her or maybe she is just playig around.It could have been anything.

'Yes i do but as a friend,' I answered .

'Ok we are in a relationship.But don't tell anyone alright,' she said .

Again i was back in my thought process.I said to myself.Man what was that? What was it? Does it mean that I'm her boyfriend and she is my girlfriend?

Once again a torrent of mixed feelings hit me.I was confused,excited , happy i mean really happy.

'Ok I won't tell anyone promise,' I said , smiled and left without looking back .That was weird i know but this is how i was back then.A weird, stupid kid.

'Everybody make way for ma man,' Baba yelled in excitement.

Remember i was 11 years old and so was everyone else .I didn't even knew how to react to a girl.But it felt good.So i went with the flow.

'What happened ? Did she accept ?What did she say bro? Are you guys in a relationship?Does she like you?,' Jon asked without stopping.

Jon talks so fast that he can easily make a good career in the rap game.It takes skills and patience to communicate with him.

'What man, she dosen't like me at all.Let alone being in a relationship ,' I said combing my hair with my fingers.

'Really ? Come on man. Alright chill out just forget her,' Baba advised tapping my shoulder.

'I know man , thanks,' I said.

I know i shouldn't have lied to my friends.But Tamanna , i promised her.So i had to do it.

Deep inside i was jumping with joy.I really didn't know what my duties as a boyfriend were but to me all i knew was that i was now able to talk to her without any hesitation.I got back home.I was smiling all the time.I couldn't even eat dinner properly.In the bed i was just thinking about her.I couldn't sleep.

I was thinking that maybe when we get older we will go to a far island
and make a house there.Run on beach on bright sunny days, i will go to hunting and fishing.And she will cook meals for us.Even thought it was impossible because the place im from.There are just huge mountains and valleys.There are islands but they are thousands of kilometers away from here.I ignored the facts and kept of fantasising.It was beautiful.

The next morning i woke and i felt like a responsible man.I felt like now i have a girlfriend and i have to give her time and make sure she is

happy.From that day the only reason i wanted to go to school was to see her .I was extremely happy.I had the most awesome girlfiend and everyone was jealous.

We arrived at the school and i entered the class with excitement.She was there sitting on the bench.It was nice to see her.I smiled at her and then she smiled back.I put my bag on the bench and headed to her .

'How are you?,' I greeted her with a smile.

'I'm fine thanks .How are you ?,' She replied back smiling.

'Good'

We talked for a while , then we headed to the morning assembly (which included excersies , prayers, students would present topics on different stuff etc).The whole day we were looking at each other and passed smiles.I liked it.It was awesome.

The school was over at 3pm and students and teachers were coming out of the building to board their respective buses.I was talking to Jon outside the building and Rihana came in.

'Can i talk to you for a second?,' Rihana asked and gestured with her fingers.

'Yeah ! Hold on,' I answered .

We walked 20-30 yards and stopped.

'You know Tamanna told me to inform you that she wants to break up with you,' Rihana said in a sad tone.

'What ? What kind of breakup? We are not in a relationship.Where is she?,' I asked .

My heart was pounding fast.I thought why would she do this ? We just lasted just for a day and now what? I had a lot of questions that needed answers.My heart sank in sadness.It was way more difficult than proposing her (that i never did).

'Everyone knows it come on.She just wants to breakup that's it .She is there ,'Rihana said pointing towards the building corner.

'I want to talk to her,' I said

'She does not want to talk to you anymore, she just wants to breakup that's it.If she really wanted to talk she would have came up to you .But she dosen't want to,'Rihana said shrugging.

She was right.If Tamanna really wanted to talk she would have came upto me and talked about it.But she didn't.

'Ok fine,' I said and left.

Jon asked me what happened and i told him the truth.He looked at me and laughed.I rushed to my bus and we headed back home.

I was sad,hopeless,confused, and angry.I arrived home.I wasn't smiling or talking much.Couldn't even eat .I wanted to cry .I was heartbroken.It felt like no one loved me.All my fantasies gone.I went to bathroom and cried. I couldn't even sleep.I had no idea what to do next.

Chapter 3 : Naz

'Heyyyy! The man with a plan, wassup my man?,'
I greeted Naz and hugged him.

'I'm fine .How are you?,' Naz asked .

'I'm Good '

'So how is everyhting going ? School , home ,
Bilal?,' I added .

'Everything is good man,' Naz replied .

We sat down on a bench and started talking about
stuff.

Naz was my childhood friend.We shared the same
school and class from the very beginning (I mean
from Kindergarten).We were good friends along
with his cousin Bilal.

They were both good guys.Naz had curly hair, was a little shorter than me , always coughed after short intervals and was a sports lover.We even shared the same tutor .

At this time we were studying in 7th standard.A year had passed by

since that school tragedy happened to me.I wasn't talking to Tamanna at all.I cut all my ties with her.But i still had feelings for her.She also did not wanted to talk to me as well. I thought she should initiate the talks but she never did.Maybe she thought the same , and we let the ego win , anyway i carried on .

'There are a lot of new girls at school bruh,' Naz
said

'There are a lot of new girls in your class as well,
you lucky man,' he added
and laughed.

'You into someone?,'I asked

'Naaa .But there is a girl i like,' Naz said

'ohoooo! Who is it bro?'

'Just a random girl from our school.Nothing
much,'Naz replied and coughed

'Have you done anything ? I mean talked to her or
something,' I asked eagerly.

'Na, nothing,' Naz said and coughed again.

'Alright ! My bro.Gotta run , see ya morrow ,say hi to Bilal,' I said and got up to head back home.

'Take care , bye,' Naz replied and hugged me.

We both headed back to our homes because it was getting late .It was summer 2010 and summers are really cool in Kashmir.A lot of people go outside to get some fresh air and to have fun with friends and families.It's just cool.

Classes here generally have two sections .Section A and Section B.And the norm is that there is a corridor between the two sections (One section falls on the right side of the corridor and one falls on the left side of the corridor).And in each section there are upto 50-60 students.The most important fact is that both the sections are usually rivals.

The students from
Section A don't like students from Section B and vice versa.I was in Section B and Naz was in Section A.Teachers generally shifted the hooligans from Sections A to B. Honestly speaking i think the best students were in Sectioin B.I'm not favouring my Section but I'm just being honest.

The Section A guys would check out girls from Section B.And the Section B guys would check out their own classmates.Because it's simple if Section A guys aren't checking out their own classmates, how are Section B guys supposed to check them out , knowing the fact that their own classmates don't like them (logic).

And talking about our Section B. Well , boy it was filled with angels.In 5th standard there wasn't much to see but we were in 7th standard and a lot of cuties were studying with us.What all of this added upto?

WAR.

There were frequent fights between the Sections.Most of the time it was about girls.

Three-four months passed by.We still were not talking to each other .We would just look at each other and then look away quickly.I was starting to hate her a little .Because everyone was making fun of me.My friends would often call me "One day bf" and it made me look like a stupid.

I wanted to do something about it.I wanted to raise myself into the highest ranks again. In order to prove myself i had to either make her my girlfriend or i had to get my revenge.Because it was her ,who put me into that situation.I decided to fake this time.

I said i'll fake my feelings for her like she did and then i do to her what she did to me.

One day i was sitting in the bus , and Jon came up running to me.

'Yo yoo yo, listen up man , did you see that ?,' Jon stuttered trying to catch his breath

'See what ?,' I asked

'Get up man, let me show you something, come on,' Jon said pulling me up from the seat.

'Ok,' I replied.

As we climbed down from the bus . Jon told me to walk silently.On the other side of the bus .I couldn't believe my eyes what i saw at that time. Everything just flashed before my eyes.Tamanna and Naz were holding hands and we talking about somethig probably about making sure that i don't catch them.

Jon called her and they both looked at us.They were completely shocked when they saw me.

I couldn't stand there , i left that spot immediately and Jon followed.

'What a hoe man?,' Jon said

'Who cares man,' I replied like it didn't matter.

I don't express my feeligns to anyone.It's hard to predict what i'm feeling and thinking.Sometimes i might not even react at all.I didn't say anything to Jon .I just hopped into the bus and got home.

Everything to me was clear now. Tamanna ditched me so that she could hook up with Naz. And the girl Naz was talking about was obviously Tamanna.

WOW!

Chapter 4 : Kate

Knowing what was going on behind my back , i decided to take my revenge
because she deserved that.I didn't had any idea what to do so i approached my lifelong friend and the best advisor in this whole world EmKay.

EmKay was also best friend.We went to the same school,same tution and we lived in the same colony (by the way Naz and Bilal also lived in the same colony and EmKay knew them well).EmKay was the chilled-out type guy.

He was a year younger than me but he definitely had a lot of experience when it came to girls.He was the best advisor .He knew Tamanna a little.I narrated my story to him .But i didn't told him that i was seeking revenge.

'Hmmmm! Listen bro,' He said and paused .

'You know if you like her or love her. Just go and tell her what you feel about her bro.Don't hide anything .Be honest.Tell her that you like her that's it.Make your job easier man.If you hide it , it will bother you.So, to know what she feels about you , tell her what you feel about her.It's that simple,'

'What do you think? She's gonna come upto you and tell you what she is feeling about you? If you are thinking this , forget it.Don't let the ego or nervousness win man.Go to her and let it all out, ok,' He added

'Ok ! I'll do it tomorrow then,' I replied , hugged him and headed for home.

The next morning i was all pumped up.I practiced in the mirror , jumped into the bus and left for school.I saw her in the class , she was talking to her friends.She looked at me with a sad face and i left.We finished the morning assembly and entered our class.We had our Games class that day and i had planned to tell her in that class.I was waiting eagerly for Games class.

Finally, it was time to talk to her after more than a year.I requested Rihana to fix this meeting for me because i guees she was her best friend .She hesitated a little but agreed anyway.

I went out in the ground with Jon , there was a little park next to the ground.
I told Jon to excuse me for some time and waited in the park.After

1-2 minutes Tamanna arrived alone .

'Hey ,' I greeted her and smiled.

'Hey,' She greeted me back .

'You wanted to talk ,' She said moving her arms back and forth gently .

She would always do this whenever we talked.Maybe there is some girl

science behind it .Who knows!

'Yes i do,ummm, see i'm sorry ok.I know whatever happens , happens for a reason.The only reason i was mad at you is that ,umm ,you didn't come up to me about that break up but instead you sent Rihana to talk to me.She told me that you are breaking up and you do not want to talk to me.I felt bad .It spread like wildfire and everyone is making fun of me now,' I said in a serious tone.

'Wait ! What ? I only told her to inform you that i'm breaking up with you that's it.I didn't tell her anything else at all.She might have made it all up,' She replied in astonishment.

'Wow! ,' I said in surprise.

'Nobody wants to see us together.I trusted her and she lied to me,' I added still surprised.

'See you want to talk , you wanna be friends , im up for it.But no relationship ,' She said

EmKay's words hit my mind.I thought man i can't trust anyone.Rihana lied to me, Naz backstabbed me. I shall accept this offer .Moreover i had feelings for her that i couldn't deny.I wanted revenge but there was something in her that was attracting me.Everytime i looked at her , a single look melted my heart away.

Tons of questions came up in my mind.I thought , well technically that wasn't a relationship at all .So there was nothing to feel bad about.Also Rihana lied to me not her .She was just thinking how i would react to her if she told me herself , that's why she sent Rihana to me so it could be a little easier for me.

Furthermore, if she really didn't wanted to talk to me .She wouldn't have agreed for this meeting.

I was confused .I decided to forgive her and start over our friendship once again.

'Yes , ok.Friends,' I replied and smiled .She smiled back and left.
She looked back when she was walking away.I couldn't figure out what it meant and i walked away too.

Once again we became best friends.It forgot everything.I forgot what Rihana did , what Naz did (and yes Naz probably knew that we were in relationship first, there was no Naz at that time).We just enjoyed each other's comapny.It was getting better every day.

I started writing her letters (yes love letters).Because we didn't had cell phones ,so i thought, well letter was the only way to express my feelings.I started falling for her.Couldn't help myself.We were 13 and we had stepped into the teenage.These feelings were completely different from the feelings i had for her when we were in 5th standard.I guess i wrote like 10-20 letters to her.

Filled with my feelings for her.And guess what she wrote back and i would just protect those letters till i would get back home.I would read it 4-5 times.The more i read , the more i fell for her.It was our first time, this was the first time i was writing to somebody and it was her first time too.

I was smitten with her.I would dream about her almost every other day (i still do sometimes).I didn't care about anything or anyone .She was the most important person to me.My feelings for her got stronger every other day.Now i was getting used to her.I just wanted her to be mine.If someone talked to her i felt jealous.I don't think she was in any relationship with Naz,i never saw them talking.I even enquired about him and her and the answer was negative.This made me happy .Now it was just her and me .

I would hardly look at the chalkboard.My head would automatically turn in her direction.She always smiled whenever i looked at her.And that's what killed me all the time. I was so much fond of her that i wouldn't even notice anyone in our class.Her face started appearing everywhere.I never listened carefully what my friends said or what the teacher said.

Whenever i watched any movie i would think of myself as the hero and her as the heroine.

Once i was watching the Titanic .And i started imagining myself as Di Caprio and her as Kate Winslet.I liked the movie so much that Kate Winslet's face and her face looked same to me.So i wrote her a letter.In which i told her that if i could call her Kate .She wrote back and said that i could call her whatever i wanted to.So from that day i called her Kate (and yes Jon did too).

We passed our 7th standard final exams and we moved into the 8th class.New class , new year and new students.This time a beautiful, humle and a sweet girl joined our section.Her name was Ekhtisam.In no time she made a lot of friends in our class and Kate introduced me to her.She was really a sweet person.

<u>Chapter 5 : 15th August</u>

As we were promoted to 8th standard,we were now able to join our school's parade group.Parade groups were the best.Because our school would take the groups to this huge stadium which was almost 15-20 kilometers away from our school , and train us for the 15th August Independence Day parades for almost 10 days.A number of other schools used to come there as well.It was always party over there.There were a lot of girls and guys and a lot of fights as well.

Kate joined the P.T Girls Group and I joined the parade group .I only joined it for her .Because it was an escape from the school and I loved her .So it was a win win for me.

Despite being kicked out all the time from the group , i kept practising.Because if i got kicked out of the group , then i would have to attend the classes without her.And i never ever wanted that.

The were a number of reasons why i didn't liked to attend classes.The top reason was that the lectures bored me.No doubt , the teachers were really good.They were like angels .But the problem was with me, i hated the lectures because i was getting incomplete information from our books.I always wanted to know

more.I always wanted to know how stuff worked.I hated mathematics and Kate , she helped me sometimes in the exams.Up until 8th standard i never took mathematics seriously because no one taught me how things worked in it.So i lost interest.

But in 8th standard i took it seriously,and solving the problems just filled me with joy.From 8th standard i loved mathematics.I'm a Physics lover too.From the very beginning i was good at science mostly Physics.Physics is the best subject in this whole universe.

Anyway , i practised a lot and i got good with the parade.I was chosen for the main group and i was hyped for it.Because , Kate was also chosen for the main event (that is the 15th August).

Took a lot of hard work and butt-kicking but i made it.Schools used to take their parade and P.T groups to the hostels near the main parade ground.So that they can arrive in the ground early and practice for a while.

Jon , Baba , EmKay , Naz and Bilal were also in the group.We first arrived at the school in the evening for some instructions on 14th August, and from there we were supposed to leave for the hostel.Girls stayed in the girls hsotel and boys in the boys hostel.I saw Kate in the school and i felt great.I couldn't talk because we were not allowed to at that time.So we boarded our buses and left

the premises.Guys in the bus were going crazy.There was a lot of shouting,hooting in the bus.It was a party.Baba and I liked Lil Wayne.So he was playing Lil Wayne all the way long (Baba, Jon,Naz ,Emkay they had cellphones with them).EmKay was sitting at front and Jon was listening some Gazals with his earphones on.

No one slept at that night.Everyone was partying.And if you tried to sleep, they will take your pants off and throw you outside.

We woke up on 15th August and we were getting dressed.Guys were exchaning Deo's, Hair Gels and combs etc.Our parade uniform included a white shirt,blue pants,neck tie,black shoes,and round green caps.We marched to the ground and the

girls group was already there practising.I saw Kate and she came up to me.

'Hey,' I asked and smiled
Trying to fix my cap.

'Hey, you look good,'She replied and smiled back.

'Oh thanks just trying to do better, you look good too,' I said

'Oh thanks, gotta go bye take care ,' she said , we handshake and she left.

Her face made my day.I was ready to rock and roll.
I looked for my guys and saw Baba dancing (Bhangra) in the middle of a Police Band .They were drumming, playing Saxophones and other instruments .

'Come on man , come in, yeaaaaayy ya ya ya ,' Baba yelled while dancing.

Jon was watching and laughing.I guess Baba was high.We called him Baba for a reason.Yes , from 8th standard Baba smoked pot.He was thin, very funny , had a long one sided hair.Everyone loved him. Despite being a stoner Baba was a genius.He excelled in every subject.

The parade was over and we bagged second position.Girls group bagged first position and overall it was good performance.

We returned home .We were happy.I was happy .

Everything was going fine between me and Kate.I was ready to propose her.But i postponed it to 9th standard.

Chapter 6 : I Hate Excursions

We passed the 8th standard and now we were in 9th standard.We were 15.
No one took 9th seriously . Because next year we were going to sit in the 10th board exams .So everyone thought that let's have fun in this year.But i got serious towards studies.I started reading Physics seriously, did a little Calculus even though it was not our subject.I started reading scientists biographies.I got interested in Astrophysics.I loved Albert Einstein.Read his theories (Special theory of Relativity and General Theory of Relativity).I wanted to know how Universe worked.

I got so much invloved that , the stuff that i read , i would try to explain to my friends.And they never understood (As expected).The second most important thing in my life besides Kate became Science (It still is).

I was ready to propose Kate.I was waiting for the annual excursion.Months passed by and finally the wait was over and when i talked to EmKay about it.He advised me to give it a shot.

It was the excursion day and i was getting ready in the morning.I dressed up, rushed to my school bus , jumped in and sat with EmKay.

'You ready?,'EmKay asked and hugged

'Yes bro,' I replied all pumped up.

'Bring her home bro this time best of luck,'

'Yes sir,'

Our bus left for school and in 10-15 minutes we arrived in the school premises.We climbed down and headed to our respective classes.I walked to my class and i saw nobody.Looked around, and nothing. Went outside and heard noise coming from the assembly area.

Students had already arrived there.I located my class line and i saw everybody with backpacks .Everybody was there, Saleem,Baba,Jon,Bilal,Rihana,Ekhtisam (she waved at me and in waved back) and most importantly Kate.

I was happy that she came that day.A teacher climbed up to the stage and instructed us about the buses and othe stuff.We headed to our respective buses line by line.Our group sat in the back seat.

Jon,Baba,Me,Rohail,Saleem , Sahir and Bilal.Kate and her friends sat at the front.As the driver hit the ignition, the whole class roared .The teachers couldn't stop anyone.

Because it was excursion and it was a fun day.Do what you want to.

'Hip hip hurray, hip hip hurray.......,' the class yelled in unison.And the buses started leaving for the journey.

I looked at teachers , they were smiling and trying to protect their ears.I looked at the other kids.Some were chewing gum, some were adjusting thier earphones and some fixing their hair.Everyone was happy.I saw Kate and i couldn't take my eyes off her.She was looking so perfect at that time (By the way she had grown long hair and always weared Hijab,every girl did).
She looked at me and smiled , i smiled back.I was preparing myself.I was ready.

We reached the spot where we were supposed to go and our teachers instructed us to act calm, be nice kids .But no one listened.We walked to the park and the scenery was breath-taking.

There were hills all around us,it was a huge park, water was running down in small channels at differnet locations in the park, there were a lot of different flowers and trees,

there were already other schools and tourists in the park, kids were running all around.

As we entered the park , Saleem couldn't stop himself, he jumped into one of the channels and started swimming.When other kids saw him doing that , everybody ran in differrent directions. I ran too with Jon.

My parents had packed chips,juice,coke and other junk food for me and handed me 500 Rupees in the morning. Jon was carrying lunch with him.We decided to share each others foods.Jon had brought chicken and rice , he also had a lot of junk food with him.We played around for some time .At noon , we ate our lunch .Now i was ready to go to Kate and propose her.

I started looking for her in the park . Jon was busy with Baba.I looked around a little and spotted her with her friends . They were moving around with water bottles in their hands.I held my spot and kept watching.

I saw a bench and i sat down , i had borrowed my elder brother's cell phone at that time (he warned me that i should protect it from water) , i took it out of my pocket , plugged in the ear phone , put it back in my shirt's pocket and started listening Bad (Michael Jackson).There was a funky guy in our class , Omar .He came up to me with his friends.There was a girl and a guy sitting on the left side of the bench almost 5-10 yards away .

'Hey , wassup man,' Omar asked and sat down.

He was wearing i guess the most awesome sneakers, his shirt was out of his pants, he had a goatee and had long spiked hair.

'I'm good , wassup,' I replied and moved a little to my right.

'I'm good.Is there something between you and Tamanna man?,' He asked.

'No why?,' I replied.

'Just asking man, did you saw her ? ,' Omar asked narrowing his eyes

'No i didn't,' I answered.

'We had fight last night over the phone man. I messed up and i want to apologize to her .You know if you saw her please tell me,'Omar said in a sad tone.

I couldn't believe what i heard.I was confused .I thought Naz was the only problem, but i was wrong.She had been talking to him (Omar) over phone? Why? I had a lot of questions that again needed to be answered.

I couldn't believe myself.First Naz and now this bitch Omar.
While i was deep in thought .Someone came from my back and emptied a water bottle on my head.All of the water rushed down to my shirt's pocket and made it's way into the phone.I got up quickly and when i looked around it was Kate with her friends.

'Are you crazy ?,' I yelled at her angrily , trying to wipe my phone (my brother's phone)

'Can't you see,' I yelled again

The guy and the girl along with Omar and his friends were witnessing the whole scene.

'I thought you were feeling down and i should cheer you up,' Kate replied with tears in her eyes.

'Really ? Are you,' I kept shouting at her and left .

I was extremely angry .I thought that i would go and propose her but it didn't turn out like that.Instead i got involved in problems again.First Omar and second my brother was going to kill me

.

I tensed up , i kept walking and found an alone bench and rested in it.I looked up and saw how much happy everyone was.Kids were running around, families were enjoying shades under trees, kids from our school were throwing water at each other.All i saw was smiling faces.And i just sat alone on this alone bench way away from people.

'Why is this happening to me ?,' I asked myself

'I just wanted to make her happy , i wanna be happy, is it too much to ask?,' I questioned myself.

While i was pondering over my problems ,
EmKay came up and sat with me.

'What happened?,' EmKay asked placing his arm
around my shoulders.

'Man i suck man, my life sucks ,' I replied with a
sad tone resting my head in my hands.

'What happened tell me man?,' EmKay asked .

'Man i thought i would go and tell her but a guy
from our class is

talking to her over phone .They even had a fight over phone last night,' I said heartbroken.

As we were talking we saw her with her friends again with water bottles.

'What really? There she is man.Should i go talk to her?,' EmKay asked pointing to her.

'No, just, no, i will talk to her myself,' I replied .

'Yo get up , teachers want everyone to gather over there,' A senior student ordered us pointing towards a couple of trees where some students were already sittings .

'Why what happened ?,' EmKay looked up and asked him

'Just go over there and you will figure it out,' Senior replied

We got up and walked to the spot .We sat on the ground and other students started joining us.

'Yo what happened man ?,' EmKay asked a student .He was completely drenched .

'We were playing in the water and this stupid kid from 8th class accidently touched an electric pole and got shocked ,' the student replied

EmKay was in the same class and he knew him.

'Really ? Is he OK?,'EmKay asked , shocked.

'Yeaa he is fine .A senior saved him , gave him a CPR,' the drenched student said.

'Man , Thank God,' EmKay replied feeling bad for his classmate.

While we were discussing this bad incident .Kate and her friends joined the gathering and sat down.I looked at her and she looked sad.I was mad at her and i wanted to know everything because i deserved an explanation.I kept looking at her.She didn't change her mood at all.She looked sad and guilty.

A teacher explained what happened and we were ordered to board our respective buses.Each class made a line and students started walking towards their buses.We climbed our bus.

And i switched my seat , i sat with my other friend Jibran and checked out my phone.It was gone completely.

'What happened ?,'Jibran asked curiously.

'Dropped it in water and now it's dead,' I replied removing it's battery and wiping it.

'Oh so sad,' Jibran said feeling bad for me.

'yes,'

Kate and other students got in the bus.Jon and other guys invited me to the back seat but i refused because i wasn't feeling good.

So many bad incidents took place that day .Kate was lying to me

again (because i never ever saw her and Omar talking in class),she destroyed my phone and a poor guy almost got electrocuted.What a bad day?

Everyone was seated and we were ready to move . Everyone was talking and laughing but i kept silence.I looked at her and she came to me.

'Can you tell him that if he wants to, he can take my phone because i accidently ruined his,' She asked Jibran showing us her phone.

She knew that i was angry and i won't talk to her so that's why she was talking indirectly to me via Jibran.

'Man she is telling you something,' Jibran said trying to figure out what was happening.

'Tell her she has already done a lot , there is no need to do anything again,' I said to Jibran in a serious tone.

Jibran was confused . She looked at me wiped her tears and left .

In the meantime the driver hopped in and started the bus.We left for school again.Everyone was busy chilling in the bus.I kept looking at her.And she kept looking at me.We were 70-80 Kilometers away from school.For the whole journey we kept looking at each other.She was wiping her tears , she wasn't talking to other girls , she wasn't doing anything, just staring me.And i was staring her.I didn't move at all .My back was hurting . Jibran was not getting what was going on.If anyone asked her anything she would just look for a second, smile a little and stare back at me.Seeing her cry was breaking

my heart.I felt bad .She seemed guilty and it melted my heart.

We arrived school.I climbed down from the bus and rested in a bench near the school building door.I saw her talking to EmKay.After 4-5 minutes she walked to me and then looked at me, didn't said anything and headed to the empty classroom.I didn't do anything at all.I just sat there because i couldn't feel my back.

Maybe she wanted to talk in person or it could have been anything.It was hard to guess.

I got up from my seat and headed towards my bus.Got in and sat

with EmKay.

'What happened ?She talked to me and she was crying .She said that you guys were staring each other for the whole journey,' EmKay said

'Yes we did.I'm tired man i want to go home,' I replied and yawned .

'Ok cool,' EmKay replied

The students got into the bus and we left for home.When i arrived home, i

was scared that my brother would kill me.I lied and i said that i was running and it accidently dropped and it slipped into the water.He looked at me and promised that he will never let me borrow his stuff ever again (I take it anyways).

The school was off for the next day.So i prepared my speech .
I went to school the next day and i saw her outside the classroom.

She looked at me and i looked at her , in an instant i took my eyes off her.As i reached to my classroom door , she jumped in front of me and tried to stop me with her arms spread wide.

'Stop ! Please listen to .I'm sorry for your phone,' She cried

I looked into her eyes and said

'Do you think it's about that phone ?,' like i didn't cared about it , little did she knew that i was scared as hell for it.

'Take mine , but atleast tell me what is wrong,' She said

Her voice , it was so hard to control myself. It was magical .She made me feel like i'm the wrong one.

'It's not about that phone, it's about you lying to me all the time.It's about you talking to Omar over phone,' I said in a serious tone

'Me lying ? Talking to Omar over phone? What are you talking about?,' She said wiping her tears

I couldn't see her cry.I was about to give up but i stayed strong.She was so beautiful man,even when she cried.

'Oh you don't know now .Great! You are innocent .I'm the bad guy here right ?,' I said

'What are you talking about ? Yes i did talked to Omar over phone .You know what he was doing ? He was proposing me over the phone and i warned him that if he ever did that again i will tell my parents.He was insisting .He was begging me.He lied to you,' She added

As usual, i was confused again.Once again a ton of questions started arising in my head.

I didn't know if i should trust her or Omar (I rarely talked to him).I knew Kate not Omar so technically i must go with Kate i thought.But how did he got her phone number ?
So i asked her ,

'So how did he got your phone number ?,'

'I don't know, i don't have a phone of my own.It's my mom's number .He might have taken it from my friends,' She said trying to convince me

It made sense.He might have, who knows.Kate
convinced me somehow.And i forgave her.

Chapter 7 : Second Rejection

As i figured it out Omar was indeed proposing her as well.So there were three guys trying to get one girl.Me,Omar and Naz.

We cleared our 9th standard and we were promoted to the 10th standard .That is the board exams class.We had turned 16 years old and my relation with Kate was way better than it was before.

One thing i almost forgot to mention is that almost everyone tried to warn me about her.Everyone warned me that she was a trouble.But i never listened to anyone.

I was blinded by her love.I remember once when our History teacher told me to meet her after class .As the class was over i went to the Staff room and she told me to stay away from her.I said i will but i didn't.

It was November 2013 and we were playing a Cricket match against Section A .Naz was their captain.For the whole day i felt like Kate wanted to talk to me.She was just roaming about with Ekhtisam all day.She seemed curious.I didn't know what it was but i felt like she wanted to talk.After the lunch break we had a Cricket match with Section A. I played as well .During the match i saw Kate with Ekhtisam wandering around in the ground.I kept on playing.Fortunately we won the match. And after the match Ekhtisam called me and informed me that Kate wanted to talk to me.I agreed .

The match was over and there were few students in the ground.I went to Kate and we sat in the park.

'Did you win?,' She asked and smiled.

'Yes we did,' I replied with a smile.

She paused for a while and said

'I want to tell you something'

'Yes what is it ?,' I asked curiously.

'Ummmm.You know .I just .Can i write it down?,'
She said and blushed

'No just tell me , don't be scared.What is it?,' I
asked getting even more curious

'Ah! You know it's.Ok. I wanna tell you that ,' she
said and paused

'Yes what is it ?,'I asked again

'I love you ,' She said and blushed.

What ? What's going on ? Is she Ok? Is something wrong? Or is she pulling some prank on me ? I asked myself.I couldn't believe myself at all.

'What ? Are you ok?,' I asked with astonishment

'I'm ok.Ye.You don't like it? Don't you love me ?,' she said still blushing

'Can you excuse me for a moment?,' i asked

'Yeah,'

I walked 5-10 yards.

'Yessssssssss, yeass oh really ? Oh my God she proposed me .WOW!,' I whispered to myself and walked back to her.

'Yes i love you , i love you too,i'm so happy Kate,'I said with excitement.

'I'm happy too,' she said and smiled .

This day was one of the most beautiful days of my life.When we were kids she just said that we are bf/gf.But this time she proposed.It couldn't get any better.I felt like i had touched the sky.The November felt like hot July .I finally won my girl all again.It was unbelievable.

I started fantasising and dreaming again.The island, beach , hunting and stuff.November passed swiftly.We went to school for only 15 days in December (because schools closed on December 15th for winter vacations).
It was the last day .I was feeling bad because i couldn't see her or talk to her for 2 months and 15days straight.We sat together in class for

the whole day and we talked a lot about each other .She told who was after her (and there were a lot of guys) and she even wrote a poem for me and i also did wrote a poem for her.

The school was over and students were boarding thier buses to head back home.She called me and took my bag and after 3-4 minutes she returned it. She told me to open it when i get home.I looked at her and it was heart breaking.I wanted to spend more time with her but i had to wait approximately 3 long months.

But if we look at the bright side i was happy because she was my girlfriend after so much hard work.

I was dying to see what was in my bag.I arrived home , opened my bag and it was so cute (by the it was the first time someone gifted me something).It was a ceramic bride and a bridegroom.It was the best.

We were in the 10th class . Me and Naz we shared the same tution so did his classmates.And they probably didn't like me at all.Their hatred against me increased even more when they came to know that Kate and I were in a relationship.So they basically wanted me to break up with her so that Naz could hook up with her.

They would often taunt me and say something
like this
'Man do you guys talk over phone? Oh wait do
you own a phone?Naz

does , man she talks to him all day' and then they
would laugh and abuse her.I never listened to
them because i knew it was all baseless and they
hated us.Her gift made me stronger i would always
see it and feel her.During those three months i
saved enough money to buy her a beautiful
present.I went to a shop , searched a little and i
found what i needed.

It was a small ceramic piano on a small base and a
waterglobe was fitted on it.It was perfect.I brought
it, asked them to wrap it perfectly and a present
for her was ready.

Vacations were over and it was time to go to school.I was so much excited to see her and talk to her.On the first day we talked normally,I gave her the present and she love it.For the first week everything was going fine.

But i don't know why, what happened to me that i stopped talking to her completely.I don't know i just left her.I talked to everyone else except her. I couldn't help myself . I wanted to talk to her but whenever i saw her i would just walk away like i don't know her.It was crazy.My behaviour towards her changed so much that i started hating her.Without any reason.Maybe someone was casting spells over me

i don't know.I could see her cry and my friends would often come up to me and try to make me talk to her .

But i never listened.

When she figured out that i was no longer giving a damn about her she broke up with me. I guess anyone would have done that.She did right.I couldn't figure out myself what was going on with me.I didn't even cared about our breakup.I was like man , i don't care.I was hurting her every day.She had no other option left.

After 3-4 months i came back to my original state.And when i realised what i did in the past months i couldn't tolerate it.I cried a lot .My world was falling apart.Unintentionally ,i destroyed my world with my own hands.The damage was already done and it was impossible to fix it.

Kate had also changed a lot during that time.Now she hated me and i deserved that , she was in a relationship with Naz , people were talking about her all the time.The way she looked at me tore my heart apart all the time.I always felt like she needed help.We were not talking to each other .But i could feel her .I could feel that she was not feeling good.I wanted to help her but i didn't had the strength to talk to her.For all those years we were together and now she was with someone else.I wanted to rescue her and i wanted her to resuce me.

We were two helpless innocent souls that no one wanted to see together .I was losing her everyday.Darkness was consuming our hearts.There was no flame left inside us.

My classmates made fun of her and i never stood up for her.It definitely broke her heart even more.She was expecting better from me.But i was always a failure and a loser.

I did not wanted it to end like this .I still loved her a lot.So somehow i brought together whatever strength i had left inside me and i went to talk to her.

'Hey,' I said

'Hey,' She replied and sighed

'Can i have your notebook pyari?,' i asked

She looked at me and handed me over her notebook.I looked back and took her notebook with me .

Back att home, i wrote a letter and apologized for everything because she deserved and apology.I wrote down everything that i wanted to say to her.And neatly placed it into her notebook.The next day i returned her

notebook and told her to read the letter inside it.After reading the letter i saw her and she was wiping her tears.I knew it , i knew that there was still something for me in her heart.She came up to me and said

'Why are you doing this?,' wiping her tears

'I'm sorry .I don't know why all of that happened .I didn't do anything intentionally.Please forgive me Kate,' I begged

'You know that I'm in a relationship with Naz and it's not gonna happen again,'She sighed

'Kate i'm sorry for everything .Atleast talk to me.I do not want it to end like this, i know you don't want it too.This is our last year together.Next year i don't know where we are gonna be.Please don't punish me like this,' I replied in a sad tone

'Ok , we will talk like we used to nothing more than that,' she said and left.

If she just talked to me , it was enough for me .I couldn't ask for more knowing the mess i made.

A couple of months passed by and we were friends again.I wanted to make her happy because it was the last year for everyone at school.Students usually migrated to other higher secondary schools after passing 10th standard.I wanted to get more out of that year .I wanted to make sure that we will always talk to each other in the future.

I don't why but i started gaining feelings for her again.I tried to stop myself but it was of no use.I wanted to win her again.What bothered me the most was that it wasn't me who was being a roadblock in Naz's path.

No, but it was Naz and Omar who were being the roadblocks for me.I was the one she like and talked to from the beginning.There was no Naz and Omar at that time.It was just me and her.Now i wanted to get my love back anyhow and i wanted my respect back.

Kate still had something for me. That was for sure .All i had to do was to make her realise that i was innocent and make her feel for me.I kept on taking to her , making her laugh .I did it all .

Months passed by and we had cleared our Golden exams .We were ready for the board exams.And it was the last day at school.Everyone had to get thier practical notebooks checked before leaving.It took some time.I had made my mind that i was going to clear everything .I went to Kate and told her that i wanted to talk to

her .She agreed and i told her to call Naz because i wanted to clear it all out once for all.No more doubts , no more drama.
She called Naz, he arrived with his friends and i was all by myself.

'Yeah what is it ,' Naz asked and coughed

'He wants to talk about something,' Kate replied pointing towards me

I just cut to the chase and asked Kate

'Here are we both today, Kate .Here is three of us.Choose me or Naz.Just do it right now , right here,'

'Come on what kind of question is that ? We are friends right ? We can be friends ,' She replied and started doodling on me knee.

'Me or Naz ? Kate,' I asked in a serious tone.

'She knows what i'm gonna do if she dosen't choose me,' Naz murmured

I felt it .He was forcing her into that relationship.He was making her to love him.She was being forced all the time.There was no way she was going to pick me.

'Why can't you guys be friends?,' Naz asked rolling his sleeves to show the cuts on his arm.

'I do not want to be friends.It's either you or me
that's it,'I said

Kate tried to balance the situation by offering me
her friendship.But i didn't agree.

'I choose Naz,' She said and took her eyes off me.

'Ok,' I replied and left.

<u>Chapter 8 : (Error 404) Love Not Found</u>

We have made it to that point of the story where you can judge between the right and the wrong. I do admit that i made a lot of mistakes but whatever happened i didn't do it intentionally.I just wanted to be happy and make Kate happy that's it.But unfortunately she only suffered because of me.

After passing board exams , there were a few students who didn't migrate at all.Baba and i stayed in the same school.The rest of the classmates left.

Jon,Saleem,Sahir,Jibran,Rohail,Kate, Rihana and Ekhtisam as well.

It was a tough time.We had been together for 7-8 years and now everyone was leaving.As we grew up , everyone started changing.
And most of the classmates showed drastic changes.I never expected that.
I thought we were alwasys going to be friends but they had something else going on in their minds.

You know what hurts the most when the people you loved and cared for show a negative change instead of positive one.

Months passed by i was trying to contact everyone.Kate,Jon,Saleem,Sahir everybody.

Couldn't get a single clue about them.

One day i was sitting on the Auditorium stairs all alone.There was no Jon,Saleem or Sahir and Ishrat came with her friends to sit there.I knew her since 2-3rd standard .

She was a nice person.
We talked for a while and unknowingly she said

'Do you talk to Tamanna?,'

'No. I don't.I don't know anything about her.You have any idea?,' I asked and smiled

'Yea, she we study at the same coaching centre,' she replied

I didn't know how to react.7-8 months had passed by since i saw her or any one of them.There was a time when i couldn't imagine a single day without her and now i was spendign eons without her all alone.
Hearing her name after so long was pleasing to my ears, it always was.Ishrat sparked some hope in me .

'Do you have her number or something ?,' I asked eagerly

'Yea, i do .Write it down,'She said and smiled

I took my cell phone out and noted her number.

Ishart was similar

to an angel to me at that time.I couldn't wait to call her.

When i reached home in the evening.I finished my work and i dialled her number(I had informed Ishrat earlier that day to tell her that she must expect a call from me).As the phone rang , my heartbeat increased .

I was trying to control my breath.I was really nervous because it was the first time ever when i was about to talk to a girl over phone, second i didn't wanted her parents to pick up her phone.The phone kept ringing.

'Hello,' I heard a girl's voice as someone picked up the phone.

'He , hel , hello,'I stuttered

'K...Kate,' I stuttered again

'Kousar,' She replied

When i heard her calling my name.I catched my breath and sighed deeply.

'Hey ,' I said

'How are you ?,' I asked

'I'm fine .How are you?,' She asked

I could feel that she was happy when she heard my voice.I was really happy talking to her after a long time.I couldn't believe that i found her again.I thought i lost her forever.

'I'm i'm ..good thanks,'I replied

We talked for a while and bid goodbye to each other.Now that i had her number there was nothing to worry about.Once again we became good friends.We talked almost every other day.Everything was going fine.I asked her about a lot of things like her relation with Naz and other stuff.And she quite shocked me.

She said that she came to school to see me but i wasn't present at that time (She was right my younger brother confirmed it). She broke up with Naz after 10th board exams.She said that one of Naz's friends propsed her and some kid from from section did as well.

And yes Omar and Naz were still trying to get her.

We added each other on Facebook and started chatting there.I cleared 11th standard and now i had to sit in the 12th board exams.I

was still talking to Kate at that time.

To be honest my feelings for her started fading away.I started seeing her as a good friend and i had no interest in making her mine again.I don't know she must have been feeling the same, who knows.One day i was chatting to her and i was trying to decode her texts (She wrote some sort of Martian in FB chat).Omar messaged me.He wanted to know about her .I hated that him like hell .I thought well lets get rid of this little runt.I texted him back

'Don't follow her man , she is a bitch'

I thought he would leave her alone.But that runt set me up.He took a screeenshot of it and text her that screen shot.I messed it all up again.I was thinking something else and that runt ruined it all.Kate got mad at me , she was really pissed off.I tried to make her understand but ther was no way she was going to listen to me.That Omar bitch , he promised me that he won't tell her anything.But that motherfucker had it planned.

Kate blocked me instantly.I was so much angry that if Omar was in

front of me i would have killed that son of a bitch.He separated us second time.

I tried to call her but she had blocked me .I couldn't do anything about it.I didn't even knew her address.I lost her again.

It was the month of December and our centre was at SP Higher Secondary.We had finished our EVS paper and we decided to wait with our friend (he had to meet his girl) near Pratap Park Gate opposite Exchange.

We were three guys and i saw Baba coming towards us from our right .I was standing and i saw a girl coming out of the Exchange street.I thought she was the girl my friend was waiting for.But as she came closer , i couldn't believe my eyes.

She was Kate.She saw me too.She was as surprised as i was.Baba reached us after some time.

'Baba look Tamanna,'I said with excitement and pointed towards her.

'Yeah yea ..yea .It's her.Go talk to her.Check out my tiger everybody, yeah,' Baba yelled at everyone

I crossed the road and walked to her.I was meeting her after i guess two long years.I felt so good.She still looked amazing.

'Hey how are you ?,' I asked and smiled

'I'm good.Who are you?Do i know you?,' she replied trying to avoid eye contact.

I couldn't believe what she was uttering.I felt like a stranger, i felt so bad for myself.

'What are you saying Kate ? It's me .Don't you know me ?,'I asked with eyes wide open with shock.

'Oh aren't you the one who called me a bitch ? Everyone one of you used me.You all are same.I do not want to talk to anyone of you.

You guys are pathetic.Just go away from here .Don't make a scence.My friends are watching,'she said trying to avoid me.

Her words broke my heart completely.I was so much shocked that i couldn't even say anything.I was numb.No one ever insulted me like that.I wanted to walk away but i couldn't feel my legs.Looked around and what i saw was even more shocking Omar and his friend (i knew

both of them) were

approaching us.Omar's friend tapped on her shoulder from behind and she talked to him like everything was fine.I never gave a fuck about these guys and now they were taunting me .

Baba and my other two friends were watching the whole scene from the other side of the road.They were as shocked as i was.Somehow i walked away from there.That was one of the baddest day of my life.I crossed the road , took my backpack out and hit it with the Park's gate.I was so much angry that i yelled at my friends .

'I'm not fucking waiting here for his bitch man.You guys wanna come i'm fucking leaving ,' I shouted

'Eddy what happened man? Is everything ok?,'Baba and my other two friends asked.

'Man i'm fuckin' outta here.Fuck everybody ,' I yelled back

'Ok let's go man .We will meet her some other day,' one of my friend said

We came back home.I cried a lot.I felt so worthless and small.I looked at my parents and my siblings .I felt so bad .I couldn't believe

what i was

thinking all the time.I was just a middle class guy and Kate she was a upper class girl.All those years i gave her , all the time i spent with my classmates.It was all gone.I hardly cared about my family and cared about Kate and my classmates.I thought they were my family.But i was wrong.

I never spoke to Kate again nor did i spoke to any one of my classmates.I never ever received any call or text from them .I realised that all the time i was just dreaming and when i woke up all those people i spent my childhood years with were gone.I was all alone all by myself.

I really don't hate any one of them.I still consider them as my friends.
I just hope that they become what they were in 5th standard.Honest,kind hearted,friendly, truthful and good people.

I'm graduating this year (inshallah).And only Allah knows what

comes next.

EPILOGUE

I hope that you must have learned something
from my story.If you are still confused about how
to win a girl let me help you out a little.You can
trust me i've a little experience.

Don't conceal what's in your heart : If you like
someone and want to say something to them.Don't
be afraid of anything. Just to to him or her and tell
them everything clearly what you fell about
them.As my friend said "They won't eat you
(unless they are cannibals)".

<u>*Be Honest :*</u> See when it comes to love.You should try not to lie .Infact don't lie at all.Be honest .Speak the truth.If you lie once , you have to lie a lot to hide the previous lies.Give your brain some rest and speak the truth even if it hurts.

<u>*Never force anyone into anything :*</u> You love someone? And he/she dosen't feel the same for you? Trust me don't force him/her into loving you.It's not good for you nor is it good for them.It's just natural .Instead try to show them how much you love them or like them.

Talk about it : If you have a gf/bf or if you have a spouse and you don't know how to solve problems in your relationship.Just take some time and talk about it.Talk about what's bothering you, what the problem is and then try to solve it.

Recently i heard something about my classmates.

Jon is currently pursuing a Btech Computer Science degree from a local university.

Baba is in Jammu pursuing Btech Civil Engineering degree

Saleem is working in a company .I don't know exactly what it is.

Sahir is pursuing a Bsc degree from a local college.

I don't have any info about Rihana, or Ekhtisam or Kate.

Notes

<u>Notes</u>

<u>*Notes*</u>

Notes

Notes

<u>*Notes*</u>

<u>Notes</u>

<u>Notes</u>

www.ingramcontent.com/pod-product-compliance
Lightning Source LLC
Chambersburg PA
CBHW071626150726
48000CB00004B/1911